W9-BBW-650

Octavius Bloom
and the House of Doom

Erik Brooks

Albert Whitman & Company
Morton Grove, Illinois

To Mom and Dad.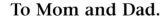

Library of Congress Cataloging-in-Publication Data
Brooks, Erik, 1972-
Octavius Bloom and the house of doom / written and illustrated by Erik Brooks.
    p. cm.
Summary: The new boy in town uses his detective skills to investigate
the scary shed that all the other children are afraid of and finds
that things aren't always as they seem.
ISBN 0-8075-5820-6
[1. Cactus—Fiction. 2. Mystery and detective stories. 3. Stories in rhyme.]
I. Title. II. Title: Octavius Bloom and the house of doom.
PZ8.3.B7875Oc 2003   [E]—dc21   2002012382

The artwork for this book was rendered in colored pencil and watercolor.
The typeface is Stone Serif Semibold.
The design is by Mary-Ann Lupa.

For more information about Albert Whitman & Company,
visit our web site at www.albertwhitman.com.

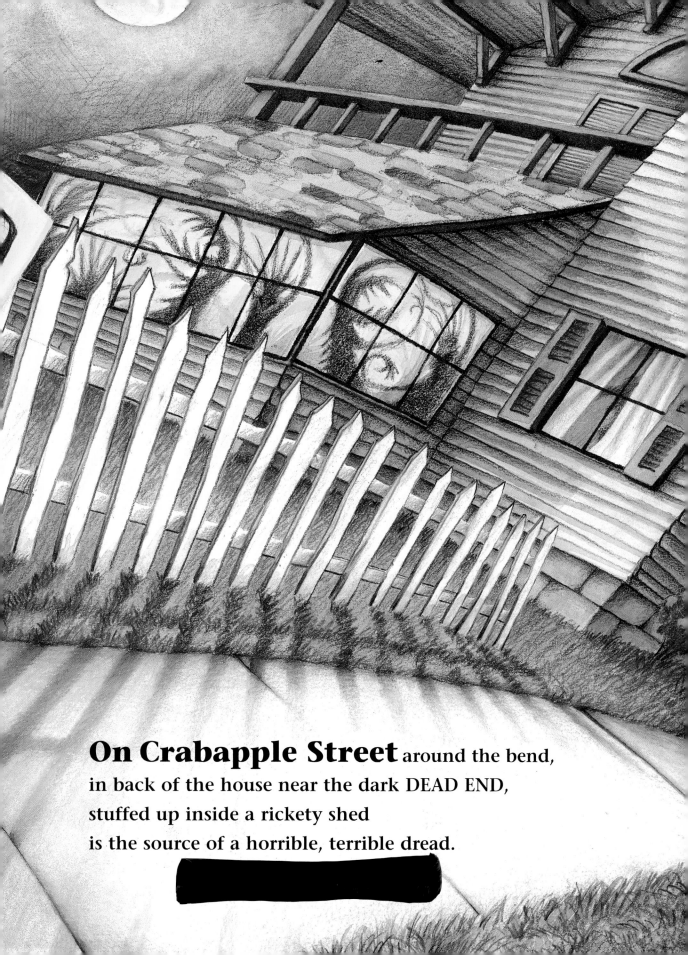

On Crabapple Street around the bend,
in back of the house near the dark DEAD END,
stuffed up inside a rickety shed
is the source of a horrible, terrible dread.

Something lives there. But what? No one knows.
So it's one place in town where no kid ever goes.
Not one has the guts to go near the front door
of the strange and mysterious Priscilla O'Moore!

She works in the shadows,

sneaks round the yard,

and her howling screams keep the bravest on guard.

Just what could it possibly all be about?
Only one kid was willing to figure it out.

"Class," Mr. M. said. "Octavius Bloom!"
And the new kid stood up in the front of the room.
He was dressed in bright clothes and had wild red hair.
His top-secret lunchbox was labeled *BEWARE!*

It was filled with things a detective would use
for snooping around and for gathering clues.
"The tools of the trade," he showed off with a grin.
"Where mystery calls, that's where I begin.
I'm new to your school, but I'll tell you the truth,
I am a genuine Pinkerton sleuth."

The class was excited, with questions galore.
This kid—a *detective?* They had to know more!
Did he find crooked villains?
                        Fight monsters?
                              Stop crime?
"Hold on," said Octavius. "One at a time!"

I'm sure there is something that makes your skin creep,
that haunts you at night and won't let you sleep."
Then one awful picture filled everyone's head—
Priscilla O'Moore's big old house with the shed!

"There are *ghosts* in the shed there on Crabapple Street!"
cried Billy K. Moe as he leapt from his seat.
"No, it's full of *vampires,*" said Maddie. "It's true!"
"Listen!" said Jimmy. "I've seen more than you.
I looked in the yard once—I thought I was brave—
hands crawled from the ground! It's a big *zombie* grave!"

Even Shirley McGee overheard a strange call
Ms. O'Moore had made on a phone at the mall.
"She bought *puppy ears!* Yuck! But believe what I say...
I saw them delivered the very next day!"
"Werewolves..." Will whispered. "They *eat* puppy ears!"
And together they shared their worst possible fears.

"OK," said Octavius. "Enough is enough.
You've given me plenty of top-notch good stuff.
I'll visit this house at the end of the day.
I can tackle this case without further delay."

When the last bell stopped ringing, he packed up his tools,
and was off to the shed with the werewolves and ghouls.

Octavius searched, and it soon became clear
that at least in the yard there was nothing to fear.
He picked up a dirty old glove and he smiled.

"What we've got here are visions of monsters run wild!
They thought that this thing was a zombie's hand.
And those 'graves'—they're really just piles of sand."
But more mystery lay behind the shed's door,
so Octavius went home to research some more.

By noon the next day he had found enough clues
and was ready to share what he hoped was good news.
"I've solved it, I'm sure," he announced after lunch.
"Using all of your tales and my own little hunch.
Come along after school. We can go as a group.
I can check one more thing and then give you the scoop."

So they waited until all the daylight was gone
and then gathered at last on Ms. O'Moore's lawn.
Octavius leaned on the door to the shed,
cleared his throat twice, and then boldly he said...

TOP SECRET

"There's nothing to fear, folks! The source of your fright
is really...*whoops!* Whoa!" CRASH! He vanished from sight!

"I'm OK!" he called out, but the others had fled.

"All right, then," he thought. "I should check out this shed."

And there, on the ground, just beside his right shoe,

Octavius found his last mystery clue.

It was shiny and green. He made his notes brief.

"Just as I'd thought!" he sighed with relief.

Then suddenly—shadows! He tensed up with fear.

A THUMP and a BUMP. Was someone else here?

"Hello there…" he called. But no answer came back.
And he couldn't quite see in the nearly pitch black.
Feeling around, he found needle-sharp spikes.
Octavius froze and whispered, "Yikes!"
He thought something moved at the end of the room
and the dark came alive in that house of doom!

He heard a door open. Octavius screamed.
What he saw was much worse then he'd ever dreamed.
A giant and writhing hairy beast
had cornered him for an evening feast!
It towered above him ten feet high.
And Octavius gulped,

"I'm gonna die!"

He dove for a corner and hid on the floor,
and the monster called from the open door.
"Are you OK?" a sweet voice said.
Octavius nodded his aching head.
When he opened his eyes and looked around,
not one single monster was there to be found.

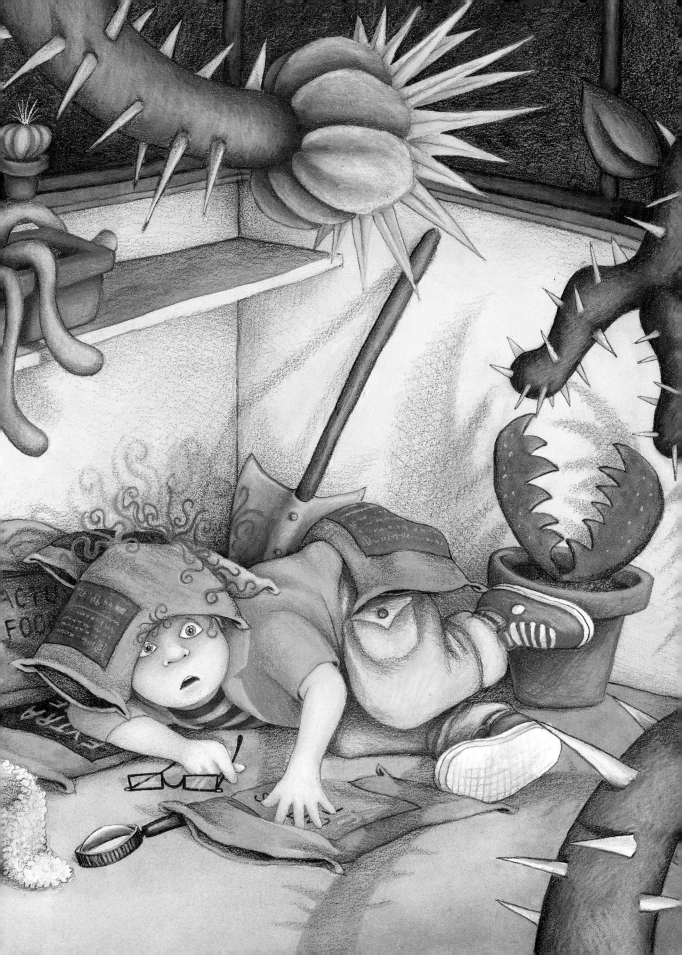

But all around were fancy plants,
and Priscilla O'Moore in her gardening pants.
"I was checking my cactus," she said with a grin.
"But what are you doing? How'd *you* get in?"
Octavius chuckled and told her the tales
of mystery shadows and ghostly wails.

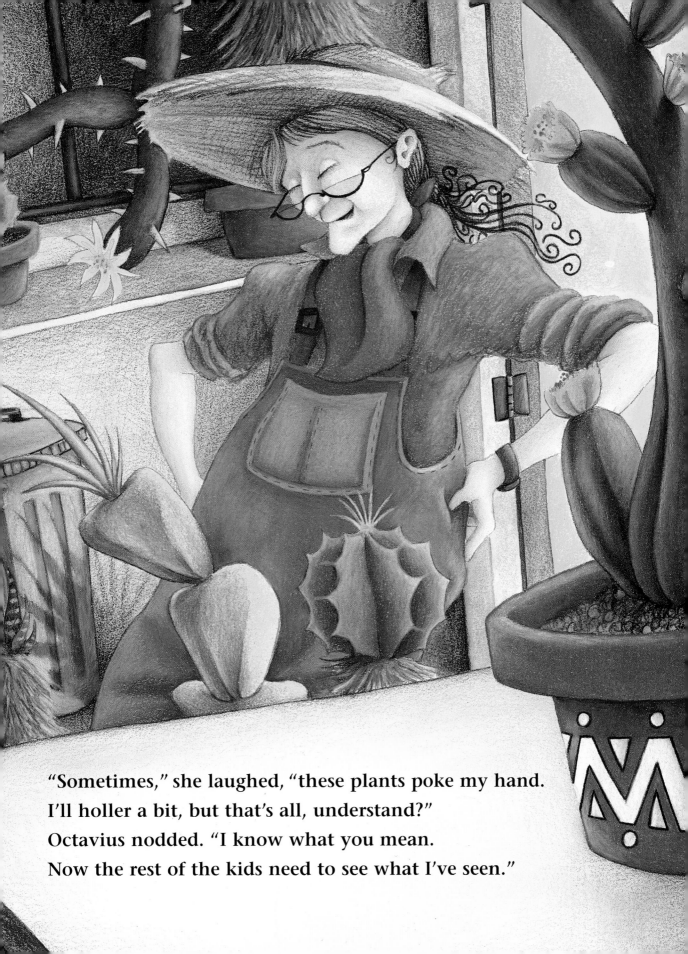

"Sometimes," she laughed, "these plants poke my hand.
I'll holler a bit, but that's all, understand?"
Octavius nodded. "I know what you mean.
Now the rest of the kids need to see what I've seen."

The others had scattered and run off to hide,
but returned when Octavius stepped back outside.
"Ahem...here's the thing," Octavius said.
"This house is not haunted and neither's the shed.
The clues that I used are all scattered about.
Take a good look around and you'll figure it out.
The monsters are *cacti* lit up on dark nights.
They cast shadows that gave you the wicked frights.
This creepy old shed with its ominous gloom
is a really fantastic cactus room!"

"Remember this fact,"
Octavius beamed.
"Things are not always as bad as they've seemed.
There's no problem in town that's too big or too small.
If I can help out, please give me a call.
Since the shed's awful monsters have now been exposed
this mystery case is officially closed!"

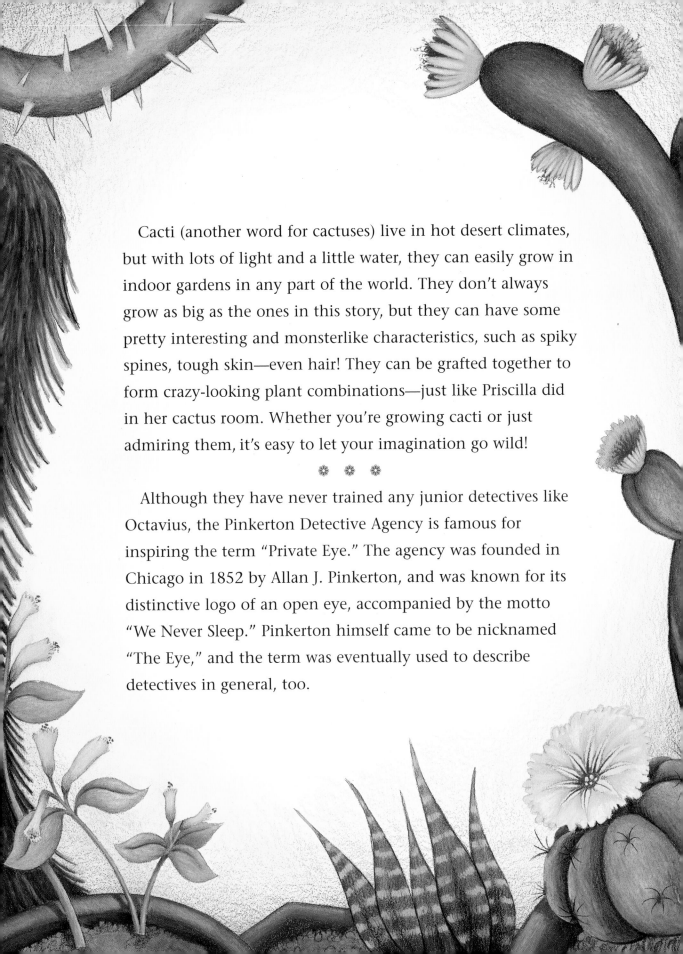

Cacti (another word for cactuses) live in hot desert climates, but with lots of light and a little water, they can easily grow in indoor gardens in any part of the world. They don't always grow as big as the ones in this story, but they can have some pretty interesting and monsterlike characteristics, such as spiky spines, tough skin—even hair! They can be grafted together to form crazy-looking plant combinations—just like Priscilla did in her cactus room. Whether you're growing cacti or just admiring them, it's easy to let your imagination go wild!

❈　❈　❈

Although they have never trained any junior detectives like Octavius, the Pinkerton Detective Agency is famous for inspiring the term "Private Eye." The agency was founded in Chicago in 1852 by Allan J. Pinkerton, and was known for its distinctive logo of an open eye, accompanied by the motto "We Never Sleep." Pinkerton himself came to be nicknamed "The Eye," and the term was eventually used to describe detectives in general, too.

JE   10/03